We Had a Window Fan

Wiley Traylor

Published by Wiley Traylor, 2022.

WE HAD A WINDOW FAN

First edition. March 30, 2022.

Copyright © 2022 Wiley Traylor.

ISBN: 979-8201891312

Written by Wiley Traylor.

Note to the Reader

This is a collection of memories, some more than 60 years old, that have been rambling about in the fuzzy chambers of the author's mind. In some instances, time has blurred the distinction between fact and fiction, reality and imagination, and softened the details so much so that even the author cannot attest to the perfect accuracy of each reflection. Regardless, it is the hope of the author that the reader will find some kinship to these memories and reflect upon their own individual lives and bring back some of their own treasured moments that attest to the absolute splendor of life.

Though we all have some recollections of things, events, and probably even people that we have encountered along life's journey that we wish had never happened or that have left holes in our hearts and scars on our souls, it is the hope of the author that all such reflections will remind us that we are all in some similar way related to one another in unspoken ways, united in an unseen bond that erases our differences and makes us kindred souls.

Incidentally, some of these memories are so precious and so deeply woven into my soul that the reader, if so inclined, will find references to these in some of my other books, listed here at the end.

Early Life

At the time, I thought my childhood was rather normal. I had a mother and a father who stayed married until "death do ye part", one each of an older sister and a younger brother, dogs (at any given time at least one that hung around the house and licked the gravy from the iron skillet), friends, a boat load of cousins on both sides, a church, and five acres of pine trees, grass, hills, woods, and a creek, that were as available as one could desire, if one was willing to fight the occasional moccasin or king snake for possession. Now, in retrospect, and looking at the lifestyle of the average modern suburban subdivision family, I think it was exceptional.

As I look at my family today, I realize back then we had very little in the way of modern gadgets and comforts. There was no water heater, except for the old kettle and pot that each heated a half gallon of water on the stove, that when carefully poured around the edge of the old cast-iron tub, would at least knock the chill off the sides and allow you to sit without undue discomfort.

Television arrived in the form of a single black and white set donated by an uncle who had moved up to color. The old Motorola spent as much time on the workbench in the local television service shop as in our living room.

Color television eventually arrived in the form of another hand-me-down but meant very little to me. My maternal grandfather was colorblind, and following the genetic passage, I, unbeknownst to me until later in life, inherited a red-green deficiency that resulted in some considerable grief as a young child. It's a bit humorous now, but while receiving the numerous paddlings in those early school years from a teacher who had apparently never before encountered a colorblind student, and who mistook my failings (often manifested in certain vegetables and other common articles of life being colored incorrectly) as instances of being a 'smart aleck', it was not pleasant. As everyone knows, once labeled, always labeled. It also explained why I was not impressed when the richer kids showed up with the big box of 64 crayons. I couldn't see what the big deal was about having so many of the same color.

But all in all, I wouldn't have traded either my childhood or my parents for any other. My parents, despite the challenges of living near the poverty level, somehow managed by the grace of the good Lord to get each one of us three children safely to adulthood. However, along the way, there were some bumps in the road.

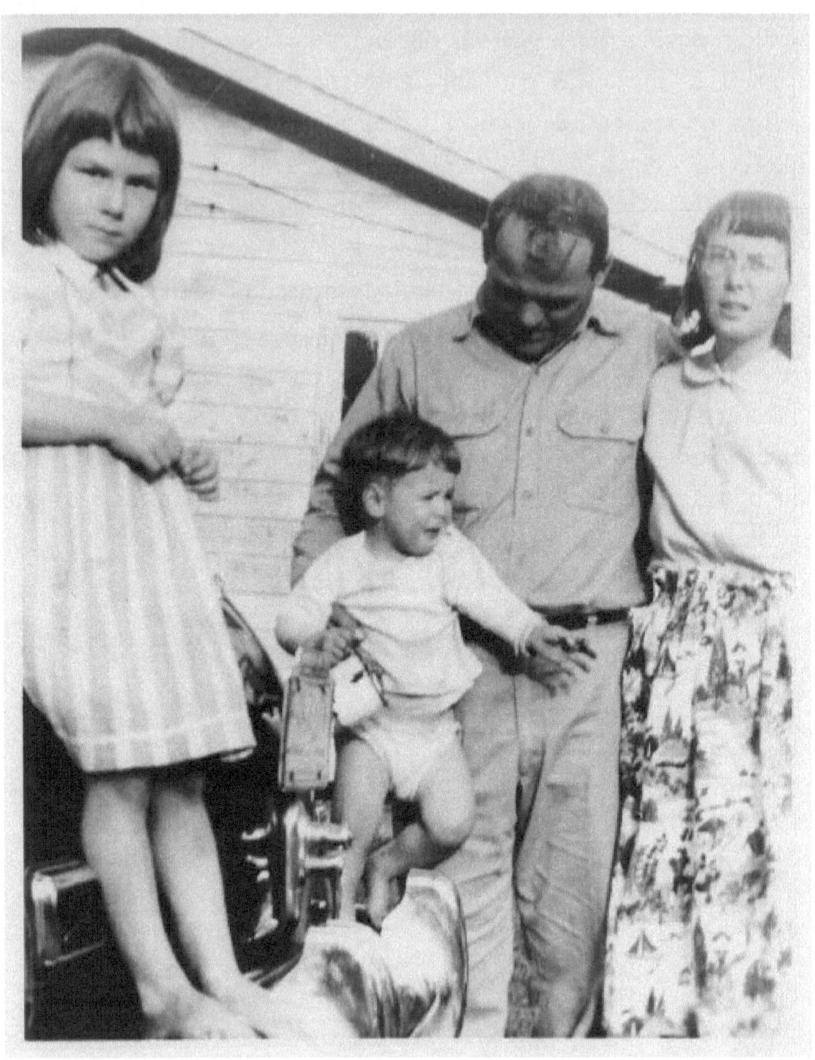

THE FAMILY, CIRCA 1953(?). One more would arrive in 1957. The author is the one in cloth diapers.

THE FAMILY, CIRCA 1958?

GRANDPA AND LITTLE brother, circa Summer, 1958.

DAD PLAYING MARBLES with someone that I would think was me, but then again, it could have been one of my older cousins.

GRANDPA AND SOME OF my cousins. In the background are the pecan trees where I often played. When the pecans fell, Dad would walk around cracking open the big ones and sharing the halves with me.

The House on Route 4

Dad had built the house in the late 1940s from timber cut and milled from the land on which it sat. The floors had cracks, the walls and attic were not insulated, and the uninsulated windows and panes of glass in the front door sweated profusely when the temperatures fell. For as far back as I can remember, one of the seats that adorned the homemade table was an old nail keg with boards nailed over its opening to complement the four chairs they had purchased early in their marriage, to provide a fifth chair.

He and family built it after work and on weekends. Uncle Charlie, who was the husband of my maternal grandmother's sister, drilled the well.

MY MATERNAL GRANDPARENTS and my parents. My colorblind grandfather is second from the left. At one time, the evidence of his color blindness (which I inherited) could be seen in the layout of the kitchen floor tiles where the color pattern in some areas was mismatched.

DESPITE ITS SHORTCOMINGS, the old house was a welcome place against the very varied Louisiana weather, especially when the south Louisiana winters settled in. Mom hated the cold—cursed it even and fought back bravely with the small gas heater in their bedroom and all four burners on the kitchen stove. She was always there, often refusing to go to church on cold Sunday evenings in order to stay home and "man the fires." The same caution that would not permit the house to be left with open fires burning, also turned the window fan off on hot summer nights.

I can recall the welcoming the old house would bestow upon young boys who would venture into the woods after school on chilly winter days and chase unseen game. Arriving at the front door, the view through the glass panes of the front door, often reduced by the hundreds of tiny droplets of condensation left there by the confrontation of warm kitchen air and bitter winter cold, would often be of a mother stirring something on the stove.

Mom was not Julia Child and in no way would have been a companion of Betty Crocker, but she kept us fed. What made her so special was that she was always there. Every afternoon as we children descended from the old Number 3 bus, she was there, standing or sitting on the porch, awaiting our return. The old house and Mom were inseparable.

WE DIDN'T TAKE VERY many pictures of the old house, but a rare South Louisiana snowfall prompted someone to pull out the old Brownie camera.

ONCE UPON A TIME, THE house had a fence that apparently could keep small boys from wandering away. The window that is just to the right of the electric meter was the summer location of the window fan.

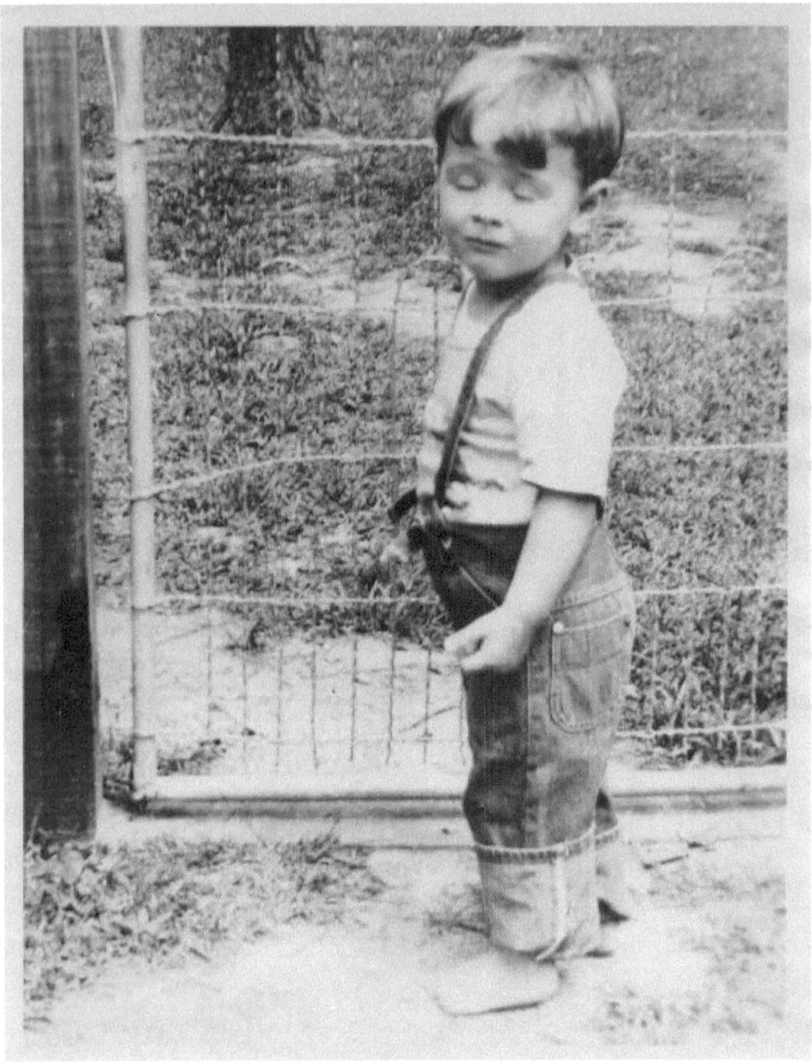

THERE WAS A GATE IN that fence that apparently made little bare-footed boys feel frustrated.

THE OLD HOUSE HAS WITHSTOOD every hurricane thrown at it, including Hurricane Betsy in 1965. It was a terrible storm with gusts in excess of 150 MPH that threw a very large oak tree down on the power line coming into our house, ripping it and the electric meter completely off the wall. The damage from the storm was extensive, leaving us without electricity for two weeks.

LONG AFTER MOM AND Dad had passed away and the children moved away, someone purchased the old house, relocated it, and refurbished it. It was a welcome sight to see the old house alive again. My younger brother had the privilege of renting the old house for a while and living there.

THE AUTHOR (FAR LEFT) and his siblings, at the newly refurbished house, reflecting upon its life and times.

An Ode to Route 4

Beneath the pines, a child is born,
    Into a land so weary and worn,
By a world at war, with all its fray,
On that sweltering, late June day.
Beneath the pines, the young child plays,
He spends his nights; he spends his days,
And when the boy becomes a man,
His play departs; he toils the land.
Beneath the pines, the young man hears,
A call to arms, the clamor of fears,
He leaves the toil, he leaves the trees,
Unto strange lands across the seas.
Beneath the pines, the warrior returns,
For love and peace his heart so yearns,
For silence from the noise of war,
For what he had the years before.
Beneath the pines, his love he finds,
A simple band their lives entwine,
They seek their place in a world so frail,
And by God's help they doth not fail.
Beneath the pines, a house he builds,
With days of toil and determined wills,
They build a home they start new life,
With this his joy, his faithful wife.
Beneath the pines, a son is born,

Into a world so weary and worn,
Once again at war, with all its fray,
One early, sweltering hot August day.
Beneath the pines, the young boy plays,
He spends his nights; he spends his days,
And when the boy becomes a man,
His nation calls to take a stand.
Beneath the pines, his parents pray,
They seek the Lord, His divine way,
That one day soon the son return,
To that place where the heart doth yearn.
Beneath the pines, the son returns,
Filled with something his heart so yearns,
For love his heart doth seek a wife,
And together they then start a new life.
Beneath the pines, the family grieves,
His life cut short, the father leaves,
All the land to his children he hath given,
Hoping together they might be driven.
Beneath the pines, the son comes again,
To seek his place there on the land,
A house they build with toil and strife,
But lived with love both he and wife.
Beneath the pines, a mother dies,
Her life too short, it breaks the ties,
For now the land holds no band,
To tie the children to the land.
Beneath the pines, all loved ones depart,
Each their own way, their lives now apart,
For without the ancestors so dear,
The land holds no bindings as clear.
Beneath the pines, the land now still,

Where none doth toil; where none doth till,
But joy and memories do so abound,
Where so much life was once there found,
Beneath the pines.

The Window Fan

We had a window fan. It was a two-speed metal monster with forward and reverse, stuffed each year into one of the windows of my parents' bedroom when the approach of summer was well defined. Its installation was a ceremony of sorts. In addition to its annual vacuuming, the prying open of the stuck window after a long, wet winter, and the cleaning of the window screen, marked the beginning of its summer duty. Ever so dependable, the application of one or two drops of sewing machine oil would signal the moment of startup. The resounding click of the old metal toggle switch started its day of rotation and the welcome movement of air. A young boy could stand before it and sing and be rewarded with the most interesting modulation of his voice.

How it worked was a strange thing to a young lad of six years. Not yet having understood the principles of differential pressure, I would often spend an entire summer afternoon creeping slowly around the outside of the house trying to track the path of the air. I was trying to determine how the wind that was blown out of the fan could hug the outside walls of the house, turn the corners, and find its way back into the house through some distant open window or door.

Despite the ignorance of how it worked, it was a welcome friend in the hot Louisiana summer afternoons. Mom would often do her ironing in a doorway where the breeze seemed to be most concentrated. The downwind smell of fresh linen being smothered by the iron was not an unpleasant scent.

On occasion, I would be granted the privilege of smoothing out a crumpled, freshly laundered handkerchief, carefully pressing it each time I folded it in halves until I had a perfectly square, flat piece of cloth. In my normally disorganized and cluttered world, it was the one symbol of something done correctly. Neatly tucked into the corner of a drawer, it represented a small piece of perfection, a small something on which I could hang a sense of accomplishment. It was a great lesson to learn.

At night, Dad had a great fear of something happening to the fan while we slept. I imagine he understood the dangers of old electrical devices, failing insulation, or the hazards of the accumulation of dust in places that get hot. For whatever the reason, after everyone was safely in bed, we would soon hear the click of the old metal switch that signaled the end of the workday for that fan. The resulting quiet would often be noisier than the sound of the motor, for through the open windows flowed the noises of the night. Crickets, frogs, the distant hound, a screech owl, and sometimes the drone of a far-off airplane soon serenaded the listeners to sleep.

There are days that I miss that fan.

The Pump

We also had a pump. It required a bit more maintenance than the fan, especially in winter. For unlike the fan, it was not retired to the back of some dark closet to endure the brutal cold of winter under a pile of discarded clothing and blankets. It was forced to tolerate the cold to the best of our abilities. When the Louisiana weather was predicted to go below freezing, a most strange ritual took place, no doubt precipitated by the fact that the house had an open crawl space crisscrossed with un-insulated water pipes.

The ritual started after the last tooth had been brushed and the last bedtime trip to the potty had been made. Mom or Dad, whoever lost the argument, would don sufficient winter attire, retrieve an old flashlight, and disappear into the darkness outside the back door.

The first step in this winter ceremony would be to unplug the pump from the electrical outlet that had been shakily nailed to an old post near the well. Then the footsteps could be heard as they made their way to the far distant corner of the house where a valve in the ground was opened to allow all of the water in the piping to drain away into the darkness. The often-hurried footsteps, sometimes accompanied by the sound of the crunch of shoe on frozen grass, would lead back to the water tank to open a valve on top of the tank to allow it to drain. In the morning of course, the ritual was reversed, and water reappeared at the faucets.

In the summer, the pump was the unnoticed friend who worked without fanfare. Occasionally the faucets would go dry, and a weary Dad would make his way out after supper to discover a fried lizard or some other poor hapless creature who had managed to find himself caught between the starter contacts in the motor at the moment water was needed.

But to a small lad of six or so, the greatest mystery and resulting fear came when the pump would come on and run during a hot summer night. Knowing that everyone else was asleep, it became a most distressful and fearful thought process as to why it was running. I knew the pump ran when water was needed. I knew there were faucets outside the house. So, the only logical answer would be that someone or something was using the water. Why were they there? Where were they creeping about? Would I work up enough courage to look out the window and see a face peering in at me?

The morning would reveal dry ground near and under every available faucet. So eventually, it became necessary to develop a new theory to explain who was using the water. Whatever the reason, it became perfectly clear to a lad of seven that there was a colony of trolls living in the ground under the house who had managed to tap into the pipes and apparently washed their clothes and took their baths after we went to bed. The theory was well supported each time the dog would bark in the darkness or be heard scrambling under the house, obviously in pursuit of some unwelcomed guest. It *was* a fearful time.

Not having the necessary courage to get up and look, or perhaps having enough sense to know that whoever was outside would eventually get their water and leave, and that the trolls would best be left alone, the mystery went unsolved for a long, long time.

DAD GETTING A DRINK from the flow well while Grandpa waits his turn. It was delicious water and was our only source during the two weeks following hurricane Betsy.

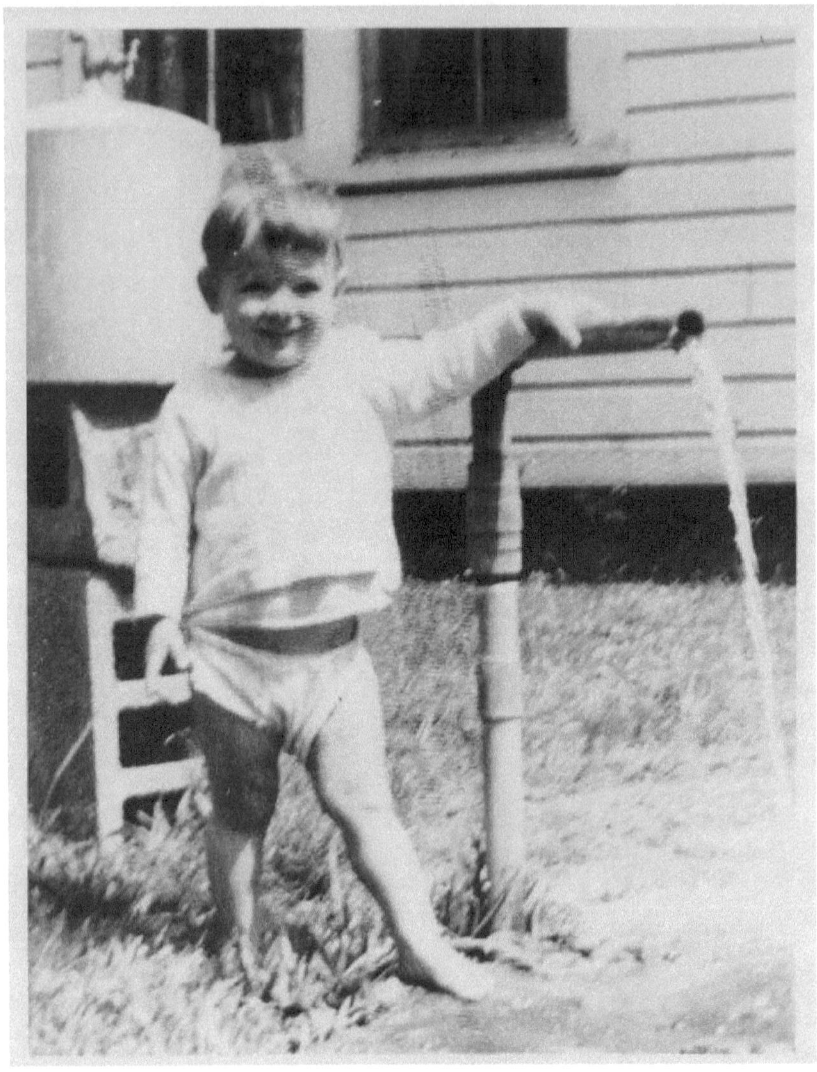

THE WELL AND THE AUTHOR, circa 1954? The valve that was the last step of the winter freeze-protection routine can be seen at the top of the tank. It was opened to break the vacuum in the tank caused by draining the system, thus allowing all of the water to drain away.

Christmas and Seasonal Recollections

I remember one Christmas Dad bought me a basketball. Not long after I had unwrapped it and left it in the middle of the living room, Dad playfully kicked it and sent it through one of the living room windows. The next day after work, he taught me how to replace and glaze a windowpane.

ONE YEAR, EVERY ONE of my cousins in the neighborhood got football uniforms. Their eager parents didn't think about a football. My dad did. The 'championship game' took place in our yard with my football. I watched from the sideline forbidden by the other boys to play without a uniform.

OUR FRONT YARD WAS big enough to fly a kite. Unfortunately, the best kite season was the month of March. If March came in like a lamb, then the latter days were best. If March came in like a lion, then the early days of the month were best. Unfortunately, despite the South's reputation for warm days, those early days of March were often still cold, and with the winds, the resulting chill factors often made the experience less than fun.

IT GOT VERY, VERY COLD one year. We could not warm up. Even with all four burners on the stove going full bore, the only place we could find warm enough was to stand on the kitchen table up near the ceiling where the warm air would rise and pass slowly out through the cracks between the boards.

FOURTH OF JULY WATERMELON was always a treat. There was a place in Albany that sold cold melons for 75 cents.

THE AUTHOR, PHOTOBOMBING. At the bottom edge of the picture, in his left hand is the source of the spot on his shirt. Mom is the dark-haired lady directly behind the author.

BY THE DRESS, I WOULD think this was one of the grand Thanksgiving feasts. The author is behind the punch bowl, with very little interest in smiling. Even my little brother managed to produce a smile. My older sister is to the far left.

THE FAMILY, CHRISTMAS 1952? The author has his thumb up his nose.

I Remember...

...**S**ometime in the early 60s I would guess, natural gas distribution came to our community. It was quite the adventure when the pipe crew came with massive digging equipment to bury the main pipe beside the road. As they laid each section, they would open the main valve somewhere up-stream and the intense blast of high-pressure natural gas would clear the line of soil and air. The roar was memorable as a cloud of dust and trash was hurled toward the sky.

Up until then, we had used propane from a large tank buried out near the well. Why it was buried was probably a testament to one of Dad's unexplained fears. I suppose Dad had seen enough of the craters made by explosions during his war experiences and wanted no such possibility of the explosion of several hundred gallons of propane reducing our house to rubble.

Dad stepped up to claim the promise of a never-ending supply of gas, bought a huge roll of the gas line, and dug the ditch out to the road to meet the newly installed gas meter. After some serious work each evening (after his hours at his regular employment) that involved cutting through hundreds of stubborn pine roots and ridiculously sticky Louisiana clay, the black plastic pipe was laid, and the house connected. There was a lot of air in the pipe, and to hurry along its purging, Dad turned on all four of the stove's burners.

When the smell of gas signaled the air had been purged, the stove was lit. The resulting flames leapt nearly to the ceiling. In all the newness of natural gas, Dad had not known to change the jets in the stove from propane to natural gas. It was a scary moment, but a couple of coats of paint covered the damage, and all was well.

...ONE YEAR WHILE WAITING for a hurricane to arrive, we found a homeless puppy out near my Paw-Paw's mailbox. Dad had never allowed animals in the house, but as the winds began to blow and night descended, I think he felt sorry for the little pup and allowed us to bring it in for the duration of the storm. I can't recall exactly the name that we eventually gave it, but it was either Bear or Guess. Mom always thought it quite clever that we should name one of the poor animals that adopted us as Guess. Here's how she explained it.

Neighbor: "Is that your dog?"

Traylor kid: "Yes."

Neighbor: "What's his name?"

Traylor kid: "Guess"

At which time she would say they would probably go through a long list of possibilities like Spot, Rover, or Lassie until they finally would catch on. I don't think most of the kids in our neighborhood were quite as sharp as Mom had expected.

...CHARLOTTE. CHARLOTTE (not her real name) came into my life at a very young age one day while I was playing alone under a large oak tree that blessed us with some measure of shade on those hot Louisiana summers. As I played, I was wishing for a friend and not long after, Charlotte appeared.

Charlotte, as I recall, didn't own much. In fact, on those days when she came to play, I now realize she always wore the same clothes—tattered jeans with a large hole in the left knee, a well-worn shirt that might have been handed down from an older and larger sibling, and a pair of those flat shoes we called "tenny shoes." Socks it seems, were optional.

She also had some school clothes although for some unexplained reason, I never saw her at school. Perhaps she was in a different classroom, or I suppose she had other friends that occupied her attention.

Charlotte also had a very pretty pink dress that she wore on special occasions. I only ever saw it on Easter Sunday morning, for apparently, as I later learned, it was the only very special clothing she had, carefully folded and guarded on a shelf in the back of her small closet in one of those flat, white boxes. It had been handed down from an older cousin and, as Charlotte grew, tenderly altered each year by her mother in those days of late Spring leading up to Easter. Eventually, there was no more material to let out, and the years of stiches and alterations had taken their toll and the dress in the box in the closet was never seen again.

Strangely enough, Charlotte disappeared from my childhood as quickly as she had materialized. I have no recollection of exactly when she ceased to be a friend and what may have happened to her, but a few years later, her brother Darby became a friend to one of my siblings, and many years later, I met one of her grandchildren, a delightful child named Kellie.

...AT HOME MILK DELIVERY. If Mom wanted a carton of milk, (not available in glass bottles where we lived), she would take an empty carton out to the corner fence post at the end of our driveway and impale it on an old rusty nail near the top. Whenever the milk delivery truck passed, he would stop, blow his horn, and Mom would trot out and buy a carton of milk.

... WE FINALLY GOT A PHONE when I came home from the Army. It was a rotary phone, complete with what in those days we called a "party line." Although we shared the line, we did have our own unique phone number and ring. I believe we were two shorts and the neighbor's was one long.

...A&P, WINN-DIXIE, AND Sunflower. Every Saturday was the same. First a trip to the A&P for what was on sale there, 8 O'CLOCK coffee, and what ever else Mom preferred to get at A&P. Then a stop at Winn-Dixie for what might be on sale there that week, and finally a quick run into Sunflower. I think it was local, and from time to time, Mom could find good bargains there.

Before them, there was a place called the Hammond Wholesale. I don't remember much about those trips there, but a couple of things stand out clearly. The manager was an extremely tall man, good natured, and kind to my parents. Mom often saved a few coins by buying the dented cans of vegetables, and apparently, being a wholesale outfit, I suppose they were the recipients of all the dented cans that the regular supermarkets couldn't sell.

I also recall it was where I was introduced to the dog with the black eye patch, the little sailor boy, and the prize inside. I think a box was 5 cents.

The only unpleasant memory of that store was the Tonka toys. Great big yellow trucks and machinery that was well out of our budgets.

...CANDY CIGARETTES AND wax lips at Halloween.

...A CANDY CALLED SUGAR Daddy. The Sugar Daddy was a thick caramel candy on a stick that was probably the number one enemy of dental care. I seem to recall someone relating how they pulled their first loose tooth. Seems it adhered to the Sugar Daddy and when they took the sucker out of their mouth, the tooth came with it.

...METAL ICE TRAYS WITH a lever. This was back in the days before ice makers were common. You'd fill them with tap water, carry them gingerly to the freezer compartment of the old Westinghouse refrigerator, and in several hours, you could have large cubes of ice. If you followed the stern directions about washing your hands before getting ice, and you failed to dry them completely, you'd be rewarded with your fingertips stuck to the sides of the aluminum tray.

...S&H GREEN STAMPS. They came with each purchase of groceries and if you collected enough of them in their designated booklets, they could be redeemed for gifts like a toaster, drinking glasses, or any number of household items. The redemption center was some 40 miles away in Baton Rouge, so it became somewhat of a pilgrimage for several families to pile in someone's car and make the journey.

...CAP PISTOLS. MOST resembled the old wild west 6-shooter. The caps were on red rolls that came in a little box. Flip open the side of the pistol's cylinder, feed the caps up between the hammer and the strike area, and pull the trigger. Great fun, magnificent smell, and the occasional hot sparks that spewed out and burned the top of your hand made for realistic adventure.

...THE FIRST POLIO VACCINATIONS. Polio was the dreaded childhood disease that kept all of our parents on the edge of their collective seats. When the vaccinations first came out, we were all herded up and taken to wherever the shots were being dispensed. I recall going one Sunday afternoon and standing in line at the high school gymnasium, waiting for what seemed like the ultimate in terror.

...MERTHIOLATE. MOST people referred to it as mercurochrome, but in our house the bottle definitely had the word Merthiolate on its label. It was the cure all for any scraped knee, cut finger, or whatever else Mom or Dad determined could benefit from an application of the hot-pink liquid.

...THE WRINGER WASHING machine. Big open tub, strong arm with 2 rubber rollers that squeezed the water out of the clothes as they passed from the soapy mixture into a big metal tub filled with clear water. It really did take a household engineer to operate the thing. If the clothes were not inserted between the rollers carefully, they could wreak havoc on zippers, buttons, or any other part of the clothing that was not designed for intense pressure. Fingers were especially vulnerable to the force, since the gap between the rollers was much smaller than the size of even the smallest digit.

...THE OLD MEN OF THE family playing Dominoes at Grandpa's house. It seemed to be the game of choice among the older generation, and any time any one of my grandpa's friends would come for a visit, the box of Dominoes would come out and the noise would begin. The old men didn't necessarily talk loudly, but they did seem to enjoy slapping the little bricks down on the table quite noisily when playing a double-six against a double four for the highly sought after 20 points. From somewhere deeper within the house would come Grandma's angry protests.

...1, 2, 3, RED LIGHT, often played at night when families visited and children were ushered outside. Great game and no one got hurt except for the innumerable mosquito bites and the resulting broken skin from children with sharp fingernails.

... CATCHING LIGHTNING bugs. Most folks know them as fireflies, but for most of the kids of the deep south, they are lightning bugs.

...THE JOHN PELA SHOW on WWL-TV out of New Orleans and American Bandstand. As we got a little older, and girls began to become more interesting members of the human race, we would often get together on Saturday afternoons with our cousins and buddies and watch the girl dancers.

...MOM'S CLOTHESLINE. It stretched from just west of the old pump out to the edge of the woods. We never had a clothes dryer at home, and after running the clothes through the ringer on the ringer washing machine 2 or three times, Mom would haul the heavy load out to the clothesline and hope for fair weather. It was a particularly miserable job during the Winter months. If rain was not forecast, she'd put them out on the line, and they would freeze. We learned that ice will evaporate and sometimes the clothes would be brought back inside, stiff as boards, but dry. When the weather was cold and rainy, sometimes she dried them in the house. Other times, we'd go to a washateria and spin them in the dryers.

...RADIO STATION WSMB (AM 1350) and the Arthur Godfrey show. Mom would break the old Truetone radio out when ironing and enjoy the presence of the Arthur Godfrey show to help lessen the boredom of the task.

...FOUNTAIN PENS WITH replacement cartridges. Once we got past the pencil and paper stage of school, it was expected that we could learn to write reports in ink. We were past the generation that had ink wells at the desk, but not yet into the ballpoint era. There were two types I recall. One had a chamber inside the pen that was filled by sticking the nib into a bottle of ink and using a lever to draw the liquid into the pen. The other used a small disposable cartridge that was placed into the barrel of the pen by unscrewing the end with the nib. When screwed back on, a very sharp tiny tube pierced the end of the ink cartridge.

...RETURNING SODA BOTTLES for the deposit. One of my earliest forms of income came from the treasures found in the ditches that ran alongside the road that passed our house. I don't recall the exact amount, maybe two cents each, but a wagon load of soda bottles, cleaned and hauled back down to the local store, could reward a young lad with some decent pocket change.

...THE DAYS OF ONE ELECTRIC outlet per room. Back in the day, for whatever reason, folks who built their own houses didn't see the need for more than one electric outlet per room. We became painfully aware of the shortage of outlets when we got our first electric toaster. That was okay at the time, because both the refrigerator and the toaster could be plugged into the same outlet. The problem became acute when Mom decided she wanted an electric wall clock in the kitchen. So, the toaster got unplugged, the clock plugged in its place, and whenever we wanted toast, the toaster was plugged into the outlet around the corner of the kitchen door.

Grandma's Magnolia

My grandmother on my mom's side had a magnolia tree. This was no ordinary magnolia tree by the standards of any gardener. It was huge. It towered over her country home and produced massive blossoms and an incredible fragrance that blessed the early evening hours.

BUT, TO AN 8-YEAR-OLD boy, it was something entirely different, for this magnolia produced hand grenades. In the fall, they would tumble from the branches like a munitions factory, complete with a short stem that could be broken off to activate the grenade. And unlike a pinecone, they could be safely and painlessly carried in any pocket or even tucked inside a shirt for especially long and dangerous combat missions to distant lands. With 10 or 12 of these, any 8-year-old bare-footed boy could survive the most intense combat and return a hero.

THE ENEMY OFTEN SET up their machine gun nests in the briar patches just beyond the reach of grandfather's lawn mower. Between the munitions factory and the enemy emplacements lay a dangerous stretch of open territory dotted quite regularly with grand pecan trees that covered the ground with a layer of defensive deterrents. To be able to mount a sneak attack upon the enemy after traversing a field of noisy, crunchy leaves was the true sign of a great warrior. And to be able to do it without crying out in pain from the odd pecan that managed to land with the point up, was the true sign of bravery.

I do not know how many enemy soldiers met their sad destinies as a result of those brave and unceasing attacks, but I would be willing to bet that there are now many more magnolias growing just beyond the reach of grandfather's lawn mower.

The Porch Swing

Grandma also had a porch swing. We had a bunch of cousins from Mom's side of the family that would descend upon Grandma's homestead from time to time. The husband of one of my mom's sisters was a career Air Force man and would on special occasions bring his whole clan home for a visit. When that occurred, all the rest of the cousins that were either living in the area or close enough to travel, would come as well. It was always a grand time.

I recall a particular evening when we passed the hours swinging on the wide porch swing and enjoying the wonders of a country summer evening. Someone produced a large bag of dried prunes and I proceeded to eat my fill.

That was dumb.

THE COUSINS ON GRANDMA'S porch. The swing can be seen to the left. The author is the third from the right. I'm not sure, but I think the little snot is sticking out his tongue.

Misadventures

I shot a bird one time with my BB-gun. I also shot my sister in the posterior and managed somehow to send a BB into the soft flesh of the underside of the second knuckle of the third finger of my first cousin. If you need the details, maybe you should ask them. The subsequent spanking I received drove any recollection of the details far from my brain and left only a single remembrance: Don't shoot people!

Anyway, the bird was a most noisy and pesky blue jay, exceedingly arrogant and extremely nervous in the presence of young boys. My paternal grandfather had fought the pests for years as he tried to grow corn and other crops that necessitated putting something into the ground that the blue jays assumed to be bird food and hoping it would stay long enough to germinate. From him, I had learned that the death of the odd bird or two was not going to impact the world's population of blue jays. Hence, they became to me what were officially known in south Louisiana as outlaw birds.

So, it is no wonder that on that warm spring day I should silently stalk one of the pests from one end of the five acres to the other. Finally, it perched itself proudly and demandingly on an old fencepost at the end of the driveway. I stealthily eased around the corner of the house, took careful aim, and sent a small ball of copper straight into its chest.

My problem was not that I had shot the bird, but that my timing was way off. The bird fell off the top of the post and unto the ground before I could beat my maternal grandmother to it.

At that particular moment, she became a most vile beast. She hesitated not in commencing a spanking followed by what seemed like an eternity of complaining and ranting about my uselessness and worthlessness as a child. If she had been more prone to violence, she probably would have searched out and destroyed the BB-gun. Fortunately for me, after seeing her making her way to the dead avian, I had quietly slipped the gun under the edge of the house that had the most spider webs. Only a 10-year-old boy would be brave enough to crawl under there and retrieve the weapon.

Grandma Hazel and the Trumpet

This particular grandmother was my father's mother-in-law. I think her disdain for me had some time later been re-directed to my father. I recall particularly vividly, what happened when he bought a trumpet for me. Everyone in our neighborhood at one time or another had an interest in instrumental music. Most of my fellow church members before me had joined the school band, so when I entered the 5th grade, Dad searched out and bought a used Conn Director for $75.00. Back in that time, that much money amounted to a very good week's wages for him. This same grandmother, who had witnessed the demise of the blue jay, still considered me to be pretty worthless. I remember quite clearly her incessant ravings about how Dad had wasted money on someone who would never follow through with it.

I guess it did my father's heart good when I carried on with the music all the way through high school and into the army, collecting several awards and honors in music along the way. I entered the army as a bandsman in the early 70s at what was at that time a very nervous time for young men of military draft age. I firmly believe to this day that my musical aptitude and army bandsman occupation saved me from certain death in Vietnam. At least that's what my Drill Sergeant told me when I failed the Enemy Detection class in Basic Training. My inability to see colors allowed five 'enemy soldiers' to stand openly at the edge of the woods and wave their red-tipped rifles flagrantly in my direction.

Personally, I think it was $75.00 well spent.

Hunting Stories

Sometime during my early teen years, my dad who characteristically worried about a lot of things, somehow put those worries aside and allowed me full unrestricted access to the old 20-gauge shotgun that stood in the back of his wardrobe. I'm not sure how old the gun was, but it had been around long enough that the stock had warped. Someone had suggested that Dad, when he was a boy, had left it leaning against a tree for a while during and after a strong rainstorm and the rain-soaked stock had taken on the warp.

It was a common occurrence to take the gun after school and venture into the woods behind my grandfather's house. At that time, there were no houses within several hundred yards and all the woods were free to shoot in any direction at any target. I wasn't much of a hunter, but the comraderies and friendships developed through those teenage years taught me a lot about safety and the sanctity of life.

NOT ALL HUNTING TRIPS were pleasurable. One Saturday, a couple of my friends and our band director decided to go squirrel hunting down in the swamps below Springfield. We called it a swamp although the ground was mostly dry, but it was very close to one of the local rivers and probably only a few feet above sea level.

Down in those woods, we have a spider that some call a banana spider. It's a big spider with striped legs that have yellow bands. They weave large webs, often spanning several feet between tree trunks. The spider generally hangs out in the center of the web, which incidentally, puts him at approximately head height of a 15-year-old boy. It is a frightening encounter when moving slowly through the woods, looking carefully in the trees for squirrels, to realize you have suddenly come face to face with one of the big arachnids.

Such was the encounter on that Saturday. Not wanting to disturb the fellow, I stooped low to the ground to step under the web when low and behold, I should come face to face with a rather large, perfectly coiled moccasin.

Instinct took control, I leapt backward and up, bringing the old 20-guage to bear on the coiled serpent and fired. The resulting kick of the shotgun hurled me backward and on my butt. I soon left the swamp, for the possibility of game did not seem to justify these two close encounters with scary creatures.

Incidentally, our band director, who was on his first ever hunt, bagged several squirrels and we seasoned hunters came away with nothing.

IT WAS COMMON FOR SEVERAL of us fellow church members to hunt together. One of my neighbors always planted a rather large garden, and as the vegetables began to mature, the rabbits would come and devour the plants. So, a hunt was called, and we got together one Saturday morning. One of my cousins had several beagles that he brought and turned loose to run in the woods near the garden.

There was a long driveway, and we shooters would station ourselves along that driveway, back far enough so that we were not actually on the driveway, and listen for the dogs.

When they got on a trail, my cousin could call to them, and they would "direct" the rabbit in our direction.

Soon the sound of the hounds grew louder and momentarily the rabbit appeared in the opening alongside the driveway. I raised my gun and fired, and when I looked back down the barrel, there standing directly in line of the sights was my neighbor's wife who had also stepped out to take a shot.

How I missed her I'll never know, but I don't think I have hunted since that day. We also missed the rabbit.

Uncle Charley

He was known as "Uncle Charley." I'm now quite certain he was no kin to me, but back then, it didn't matter. He owned a Texaco station that was situated along one of the roads we traveled to get to Grandma's house. It was classic: solid wood floors that squeaked with each step, long wooden shelves with commonly used household items for sale, a rather well-equipped candy shelf and very cold and delicious bottled soft drinks. Any time we stopped there, it was special.

Off near the end of his property was a small white shed that for most of the year sat closed and alone. It didn't go unnoticed, for every time we passed Uncle Charley's, a pair of intensely brown eyes peered steadily through the window of the old Oldsmobile (or was it the Ford), longingly hoping to see if the hinged front might happen to be propped open. For inside this small world was the best supply of fireworks a small boy could hope for. In particular was something called a Texas Buster.

There was nothing else like it in my little world. Bigger and bolder than a cherry bomb or a silver salute, it had the capacity to turn any south Louisiana fire ant mound into a crater. At five for a quarter, it was worth any amount of yard work necessary to secure fifty cents. They came complete with a penny box of matches, safely tucked into the bottom of a small brown bag. It was like owning a sack of gold.

Texas Busters were never used like any regular firecracker. To light them and toss them indiscriminately would have been a dishonor to it and disrespectful of its power and authority. No, this thing had to be planned and well planned at that.

In the excitement, the first might be strategically placed atop an old fence post just to announce to the world that explosives had arrived and to be reminded of the awesome power of that red cylinder. But after that, careful and deliberate deployment was essential, for now there were only nine left.

The Louisiana fire ant is a dreaded beast. Any young boy can tell you the agony caused by ignorantly allowing oneself to be overtaken by the fierce fiends. Therefore, anything they might receive in return was always justified. The largest mound would be found, and the Texas buster pushed deeply into the soft dirt until just the tip of the fuse was visible. A quick light and a quicker retreat were always in order. The resulting crater was magnificent. Now there were eight left.

A Texas Buster could launch a tin can several dozen feet into the air if properly staged. That left seven.

Did you know that a knothole in a tree might be the entrance to a long hollow section of trunk that would spew pieces of leaves and bits of rotted wood out into the atmosphere? Now there were six.

A Texas Buster will explode in a cow-watering trough and get everyone wet. Five.

A rotten stump is no match for explosives. Four.

A wet cow patty is not a good thing to send through the air in every direction. Three.

A Texas Buster shot high into the air with a slingshot will stampede nearby cattle. Two.

At this stage of the game, depending upon how close the sun is to its place below the horizon, target selection becomes either highly selective or panicky. How can the last two be best used to produce the most joy (damage)?

Red ants don't know how to surrender and apparently, some can survive the blast of a Texas Buster, be blown halfway across the yard, and still manage to find the soft flesh of a 10-year-old ankle.

The last two exploded simultaneously. The grass no longer grows on that spot in the yard. Ants have given up trying to live there too.

Go-Karts and Learned Lessons

I prayed for a go-kart. Day after day, I asked God, however mysteriously, to allow such a device to appear in my yard. I envisioned all kinds of scenarios whereby the coveted machine would show up. As I got older, I realized that God was not in the go-kart business, and I had pretty much resolved myself to the fact that it would never happen.

One summer during the troubles of the late '60s, my grandmother decided she would return to the land of her early life for a visit and made arrangements to spend several weeks with her children who lived in California. Fearful that something might happen to her unoccupied home up in the sticks, she convinced my father and mother to live there while she was away. So, we moved into the house and took up residence.

It was a wonderful summer. My grandfather had a collection of tools he had gathered over some 60 or so years of living, a massive number of bolts, screws, heaps of metal scraps, and old wheelbarrow wheels and such that turned out to be just the thing from which a young lad could assemble something with wheels.

I worked most of the summer and eventually put together a version of the coveted go-kart. It was powered by a very old gasoline washing machine motor with a push-kick starter. (Yes, back in the days before rural electric power, washing machines, which were often located in an out-building, were powered by gasoline engines.)

IT DIDN'T HAVE MUCH power, but with the right pulleys, a favorable ratio was finally obtained that allowed it to carry me down the long driveway and back. It wasn't until many years later that I realized God had answered my prayers for a go-kart by giving me the aptitude to put one together. Though it wasn't as fast and elegant as a store-bought machine, I think the skills I learned that summer were much more valuable.

IT WAS ALSO DURING this time that I learned to drive. My grandparents had an old Nash Rambler that I would sneak out of the barn and run up and down their extra-long driveway. The frequent starting and short runs eventually took their toll on the battery, which necessitated a confession to my dad, and a subsequent shutdown of my driving adventures.

The Store

Howard had a country grocery store. He also had a tractor, and a cigar. The tractor made far more smoke than the cigar. In fact, the cigar made no smoke at all for he never lit it. He would keep it in his mouth and through a gloriously developed set of Masseter and Buccinator muscles, he had perfected a sort of masticatory performance that could roll and move the cigar simultaneously from one corner of his mouth to the other without missing either a single spoken word or a breath. Somehow, it was linked to some cranial activity that manifested itself in a rapid movement from one side to the other during various activities. While riding on his tractor for example, the cigar could be seen moving from one side to the other every three or four seconds. Not being plagued with the danger of setting himself on fire, it mattered very little to him on the rare occasion that he may have inadvertently forgotten that it was there and allowed it to drop to rest on his ample torso while slipping off to sleep in his favorite chair in the corner of his country store.

But alas, I digress. The Store, as it was known, was just slightly over one-half mile from my childhood home. I can remember days when my mother and I would walk there for the sole purpose of picking up a carton of milk or maybe a loaf of bread. Getting there on a hot Louisiana summer day was not a pleasant experience and to make matters worse, unlike Uncle Charley's, Howard's store had the candy rack in full reach of even the youngest toddler. Though I never considered him a very astute businessman, I now can see that placing the candy within such easy reach of any soon-to-be-crying toddler was probably good for business. Unfortunately, for me, it was only good for tears.

In the company of my mother, the store held little value for me. It was a destination; a place in space and time that needed to be visited from time to time for reasons that I did not know at the time. But as I look back, knowing now as an adult what I have deduced from what life demands of parents, I suspect it was more likely that Howard's store was a place of last resort. Typically, his products were more expensive that one could find by traveling into town to the A&P or Winn-Dixie. However, for the one-off item, it made much more sense to go to The Store than to make the journey to town. It also seems likely, knowing now that we were living on very limited income, that The Store may have represented the most economical option available to a mother who had neither automobile nor license to drive and only coins in her purse.

But there was a bright spot to these trips to the store. Her name was Mrs. Cunningham. She was a frail older lady with white wispy hair that lived in an extremely modest house tucked nearly out of sight in the woods across from Jerusalem Baptist church. She had vanilla wafers and a kind of indescribable affection for people who would take the time to visit her. I can remember sitting on the stoop of her front door with a modest fistful of cookies while she and Mom visited.

As I grew older, Mrs. Cunningham somehow disappeared. I suspect she passed on to her much deserved reward; but unfortunately, for me, it passed without my recognition. I suppose I had outgrown the vanilla wafers and hence (to my shame) the interest in Mrs. Cunningham.

When I outgrew the need for Mom's hand to escort me to The Store, its place in life changed. It became the spot to meet friends after school for an RC Cola and a Moon Pie. Yes, they are real and many a young lad has spent a glorious afternoon sitting outside on the breadbox, talking with friends, and enjoying the best of life. What made it sweeter yet was that it could all be experienced with about 11 cents.

Nevertheless, even the best of life was to change. As I grew older still, The Store simply became the place to get gasoline for the lawnmower, fuel for a borrowed tractor, or possibly a quick soda to burst the thirst of a hot summer day. It grew less and less a part of my life. I have long since moved from there, but I still find myself when driving about in the countryside, looking carefully at old wooden buildings with rusty RC Cola signs and dilapidated breadboxes, wondering about the good life that might have taken place there. Maybe one day, I will find one still open with an old man and his cigar sitting in his favorite chair in the corner.

The Paternal Side of the Family

The couple on the left are my paternal grandparents, affectionately called Maw-Maw and Paw-Paw (pronounced just like you'd think an 8-year-old bare-footed boy would say it). The siblings are arranged left to right by age. Dad is the one with folded hands and glasses.

Maw-Maw's Magic Coffee

My father's mother was called Maw-Maw by most of us grandchildren. I have no idea how that came to be. I do know that 'grandmother' was too formal, 'granny,' much too frail.

Anyway, Maw-Maw made magic coffee. She made it in a sock. A sock she made from a sack. A sack she got from Jack. Before I go too Seuss on you, let me explain.

Jack Bahm had a feed and seed store and Maw-Maw had chickens. She bought her chicken feed from Jack, which came in a fifty-pound linen sack. When the chickens had consumed all of the feed, she would use the sack as material for various repairs and items, including a sock that she sewed around a wire frame that sat on the brim of an old, chipped porcelain coffee pot. The process for making coffee was quite simple; she heated water to a boil in a big blue kettle, added a large handful of ground EIGHT O'CLOCK coffee to the sock, and then poured the boiling water to the top of the sock. In a few minutes, she had a pot of hot magic coffee.

What made it magic is that it could draw pre-teenage boys from their slumber on Saturday mornings. I guess it wasn't the coffee alone, but the scent of fried eggs and bacon that drifted through the house to the spare bedroom where my cousin and I would stay on certain Friday nights. We were drawn there by the lure of gainful employment. Paw-Paw owned a small daylily farm and would, often out of necessity and a sympathetic heart, hire us to help him with planting, weeding, or other such tasks. He expected early risers and to facilitate that, we would often stay over the night before.

I have never understood how my grandparents could find the inner strength to rise before dawn so many mornings in a year. I have always tended to be a bit on the lazy side, excusing my defiance of the "early to bed, early to rise..." proverb by claiming that I was more productive in the afternoons. However, any farmer can tell you that the South Louisiana afternoon heat was not conducive to farming and in fact, the early peace and calm of the morning coolness was indeed the most intelligent choice.

Whatever the reason, they were always early risers, so when we were at their home, it was expected that we would also "get up with the chickens." Maw-Maw's coffee and breakfast sure made it enjoyable.

Maw-Maw's Drawers

Don't go all crazy and think underwear when I mention Maw-Maw's drawers. She called those step-ins. (Step-ins were a late 1920s term that described ladies' underwear that resembles the modern panties. They differed greatly from the prevailing fashion in that they did not button or require drawstrings like a corset. To dress, one simply "stepped" into them.) A smile crosses my lips when I recall a certain spanking my cousin and I received after church, brought on as the result of uncontrollable giggling over the name of the composer of the tune of the hymn, *Have Thine Own Way, Lord*.

But, Maw-Maw had interesting drawers, nonetheless. There are three that come readily to mind. The first being the drawers on the old Singer (or was it a White) treadle sewing machine. They contained a wonderland of bits and pieces that accumulated from years of sewing and mending of clothing. Folks that endured the Great Depression collected and saved everything, especially buttons and such. Maw-Maw's collection did not disappoint. As she approached her older days, I was often called on to thread the machine, un-knot the various bits of thread that fell victim to the "knot demon" who played mischief in ladies' drawers when they were not wrecking their havoc on children's Christmas decorations.

The second drawer of particular interest was any one of the six in that old desk that occupied its position on the east wall of one of the back bedrooms. It was primarily filled with the odds and ends that apparently fell from the pockets of the man of the house. Paw-Paw had worked many years for the Highway Department as some type of sign crew foreman. He was responsible for installing roadside signs like stop and yield signs. When erecting a sign, it was the practice to write the date of installation on the back in an indelible crayon. The drawers were well littered with the remains of those that were slipped into the pocket instead of left in the truck.

The primary evidence of the origin of the contents of the drawers was the prolific bits and pieces, odd leaves, and such of the chewing tobacco that was Paw-Paw's constant companion. There are stories to be told about the effects of a plug of Day's Work on the digestive systems of young boys who steal, but that should be left for another time. The aftermath left the details a bit hazy. Young boys are quick to dismiss the reality of death by tobacco and hence suppress such thoughts and recollections.

But the most interesting and attractive drawer to a young lad was the one just to the right of the sink, near the refrigerator. Within that drawer lay a virtual kaleidoscope of odds and ends. It seemed the drawer had no limit to the depth of its contents. One could find anything there from a screwdriver and screws, nails, old pocketknives, and razor blades to string, matches, and a mousetrap or two, replete with a scrap or two of the fur of the unfortunate victims.

I was often caught investigating (snooping) the treasures and reprimanded. For whatever reason, when asked about the contents, they referred to them as "lay-over-catch-meddlers." It remains a pleasant thought. This might explain why there are such drawers in all of our lives.

Sputnik

Paw-Paw owned a dog. Or perhaps a dog owned Paw-Paw. I'm not sure how the relationship came to be, but I do remember it was a Spaniel with a serious attitude. I assumed it was named after the Russian satellite launched in 1957, but the exact details escape me at times.

It hated nearly everyone who ventured into the yard. It would often snarl uncontrollably from within the dark recesses under the front porch. Though unseen, there was no doubt about the presence of the beast. The fact that it could launch out at any moment and tear a human leg to shreds made it even more hideous.

Before you think this just unsubstantiated fear unjustifiably embedded in the heart of a young boy, the proof of his savagery could be found occasionally scattered about the yard in the early hours of morning. On more than one occasion, the mangled remains of a possum or skunk had to be drug off and tossed into the creek.

But Sputnik had a split personality. It was quite tolerant of my own father, though Dad never vividly expressed any fondness toward it. But the real mystery was the obvious and abundant affection Sputnik displayed for my cousin Bill. When Bill would enter the yard, dog and boy would meet like old friends. The dog's tail would wag so violently that it bowed the dog from just behind the front legs all the way to the tip of its tail. To this day, I guess I remain a bit envious of Bill.

Paw-Paw's Christmas Lights

Paw-Paw had a string of Christmas lights. Now before you scoff at the idea of a child's amazement at a string of Christmas lights, let me explain the life of a small boy in the late '50s in southern Louisiana. Money did not grow on trees. I know, because I was told several thousand times by people who had no cause to lie to me, nor who exhibited any lifestyle that they had plenty of it and just wanted *me* to be poor. Our own personal Christmas decorating was pretty much limited to two 7-bulb strings of lights hung carefully around two or more pine saplings tied together to resemble a Christmas tree. Added to the mix was a sack full of those string icicles that had been used for years that somehow found it necessary each summer to knot themselves together in such a way as to delay as long as possible, the onset of the Christmas festivities.

So, you can imagine the delight of small children to discover one cool November day that the sound of hammer on nail was the preparation for the annual stringing of the lamps. These were not your average Christmas lights. These were C-9s, and each string blinked independently! They were the king of Christmas lamps!

When they came on at night, darkness fled like a frightened rabbit. The whole front yard became awash with colors dancing from bush to bush and across the front fence. Even the front of the house took on a kaleidoscope effect and the alternating blinking lamps caused the shadows from the porch posts to dance about as if driven by some uncontrollable urge to celebrate the season.

YOU CANNOT IMAGINE the comfort those lights brought to a young lad, lying awake in a completely darkened room; to look across the yard and down the road and see the colors of Christmas, flickering, blinking, ever glowing as if Christmas would never end. I miss my grandfather. It also saddens me that my children cannot be impressed by such simplicity. The gigabyte computers with high intensity games have all but chased away the simpler pleasures of life.

Leap-n-Leaner

Both of my grandfathers had life-long affections for all things with an engine. From tractors to trucks to automobiles, if it had wheels and could travel, they had one.

My maternal grandfather had a large barn into which was stuffed an old Model T, which we grandkids drove around over the rough ruts of a long unused strawberry patch, a Ford 8N tractor, and an old International Harvester truck that often came to our house and picked us up to bring us to his house to spend a warm summer day. The bed was rusted out and it was always great entertainment to see the roadbed directly below our feet as we skimmed along at the breakneck speed of 35 MPH.

My paternal grandfather (Paw-Paw) had a host of vehicles throughout his lifetime, including a Model T, a Cub tractor that he and his sons rebuilt from the ground up, and a Ford. To be more exact, a 1953 brown Ford Custom, 6 screaming cylinders, four doors, and a 3-speed on the column. I can't recall if it was light brown or dark brown.

It had two speeds: full throttle and coast. It was affectionately named "Leap-n-Leaner" (some say the name was Leapin' Leaner) by those who witnessed its passage down some country road. Paw-Paw would accelerate until he reached a speed that made it difficult to keep the thing between the center of the road and the ditch. Then he would let off and coast until such time as he got bored with the slower speed and then he would repeat the cycle. Heaven help the occupants if the coasting phase did not correspond with the curves in the road.

For a lad of eight or nine, this was a carnival ride on four wheels. There were no seat belts in those days, and you could slide from door to door sideways across the back seat as he swung around the curves. On the straight-aways, you could hang on to the partially lowered rear window and enjoy the thrill of the wind in your face and the spectacle of any startled pedestrians or livestock that happened to be a bit slow in moving out of the path. I can't remember if the windows wouldn't roll all the way down, or if they were lowered only halfway by some concerned parent, thinking that the half-closed window might somehow keep an 8-year-old boy from becoming an airborne object around one of the full-throttle curves.

I do recall one day when the ride was not a joy. I had been sick with some kind of intestinal disorder that after the 5th day had left me quite weak. Fearing that I might be in serious trouble, mom secured a ride to the doctor's office with Paw-Paw. The full-throttle-coast travel only made it worse. By the time I made it to the doctor, I recall collapsing in the hallway from the nausea.

Paw-Paw used the car like a truck. He had started a daylily farm after his retirement from the highway department, and wanting to keep expenses to a minimum, he had refused to buy a truck. He would often travel to Mississippi to buy plants and would bring home as many as he could in the trunk of the Ford.

It was easy to tell when Paw-Paw was coming home with a load of newly acquired treasures as the rear bumper skimmed along just inches from the surface of the road. Eventually, "Leap-n-Leaner" began to sag all of the time. I don't know if it was because he had over stressed the suspension, or if it was just from the sheer weight of years of accumulated soil from the plants. Then again, in reality the old Ford was just tired.

Paw-Paw also chewed tobacco. Day's Work was the brand, and you could find bits and chunks of the partially used plugs all around the house. One of his favorite places to chew was in the car. Here's a bit of information for those of you who have never known a chewer: Chewers spit. And when they are driving, they don't use a cup or old can to catch the airborne stream of brown liquid. The open window becomes their spittoon to the world. Perhaps this is the real reason the rear windows were not rolled all the way down. It also might explain why sometimes it appeared that the car was dark brown. I guess it depended upon which side of the car you were viewing.

Later on, I learned the old Ford was not light or dark brown, but actually green. I guess I was confused by the ever-present layer of daylily soil covered over by dark brown tobacco juice on the driver's side and my inherited red-green colorblindness.

Eventually he replaced "Leap-n-Leaner" with a yellow Ford Galaxie 500 with a V-8 and automatic transmission. I never rode with him in that car. Just the thought of eight cylinders under full throttle on the old country roads was more thrill than I thought I could handle.

ONE OF MY OLDER COUSINS (daughter of Dad's only sister) and one of Paw-Paw's earlier automobiles.

Great Grandfather William

There was something a bit devious about the men on my father's side of the family, especially those directly in his ancestral line. My great grandfather was feared. I feared him. I have only a few memories of him, all of which seem to include me being nestled as closely as possible to my father's bosom. In those few moments that he could somehow coax me away from that protection, I recall him coming at one or both of my ears with an open pocketknife. It was always accompanied with his complaining about how tough my ears were while he sawed back and forth with the backside of the blade. Somehow, the squirming and crying of a small boy must have given him some enjoyment. If it was his way of expressing love, he needed some lessons.

THE MAN WITH THE POCKETKNIFE and a fetish for young ears. The hand in the pocket is probably holding that knife.

MY OTHER MEMORY OF him was his death or more precisely, the wake that took place at his home. I guess I could look up the date (January 13, 1958) and know precisely how old I was at the time, but for some reason, the most vivid memory from that day was of me striking my first match. Several of us boys were playing in the street, and someone had given me one of those large kitchen matches that back in that day could be struck on anything, including a boy's zipper. It was quite a spectacular thing to see it blaze into flame and burn in my small, shaking hand. I guess it must have been a very similar experience for the first human who discovered fire.

I SAID WE WERE IN THE street, but in actuality, it was a gravel road. Well, I say gravel, most of the time it was little more than dirt. We had a political body for the parish in which I lived (county for all other states) known as the police jury that would send a road grader out several times a year to scrape away all of the washboard bumps, and level the south Louisiana rain-created potholes. It was always quite an experience for the neighborhood boys to tag along behind that beastly machine and watch the magical transformation that took place as a result of the contact of that angled blade with the road. Low and behold, some gravel would magically reappear and give us the appearance of a really smooth road.

Panthers and Other Facts of Life

Well, across that road and down a bit lived my grandfather. He was not nearly so quick to induce pain. He preferred a more indirect approach, often waiting until darkness had descended before sending fear into the timid heart of any young lad who happened to have stayed too long at his house.

There had always been rumors and insinuation that panthers lived in the woods on the other side of the small creek that ran just past his house. It was at these times when I was destined to walk home alone that he would take the opportunity to remind me of this fact. He was particularly articulate about reminding me that these wild animals preferred to drop down out of tall trees unto their prey. Well, between his house and my own, stood the tallest pine tree on five acres. It stood majestically next to the path that led from his house; big, strong braches capable of supporting the weight of large animals hung over the path that I would need to travel to return to the comfort and safety of home.

As soon as I could stand his warnings and precautions no longer, I would leap from his porch and with all of the speed of a young lad running for his life, pass under that tree as quickly and silently as possible. It was a bumpy run, fraught with the dangers of rocks that had somehow magically risen to the surface of the dirt road, sharp pinecones, roots that had long since lost their protective cover of dirt, and the inevitable odd stick or two that had dropped from some old limb of one of the other pine trees. Having safely arrived at home, I would be greeted by the warm smile of a parent who knew what had just transpired.

As I grew older, I learned that panthers were not a real threat. I became quite certain that it had all been lies just for scaring small boys until one night several years later while driving home from a date, the largest black cat I had ever seen in my life bounded across the road in my headlights, moving easily from one side to the other with a single touch of his feet.

Perhaps my grandfather really did care for me.

Church Life

My parents spanked. For that matter, other parents spanked. If you got a spanking from someone else's parents, you were even more likely to get a second spanking sometime later from your own parents when they found out. The village was raising the children long before any politician thought it would be a cute phrase to use. But the village in my case was the local Baptist church. Since nearly everyone was related in some sense or the other, it was more of an extended family spanking. I guess it was acceptable, because nearly everyone had a universal understanding of the difference between right and wrong behavior.

It centered mostly on cutting up in church and probably more precisely the nature of respect, or lack thereof. If there was distractive activity coming from a pew full of boys, we all got the spanking without any jury of peers trying to figure out who was the cause.

It taught me that if you don't have the privilege of explaining that you were an innocent victim who just happened to be in the presence of other mischievous boys but not actually misbehaving yourself, then perhaps the smart thing was to learn to avoid those who are engaging in questionable conduct. In order for that to work, it became somewhat imperative to learn as quickly as possible the difference between what was right and what was wrong.

Before you get all up in arms about kids getting spankings, consider the fact that those who were doing the spanking had pretty much just ended a world war a few years back, a war that possibly may not have come to pass if a certain Austrian parent had spanked a certain Austrian boy a little more frequently.

I believe they clearly understood that the very future of the nation depended upon raising a generation that could tell the difference between right and wrong, and that any generation that would break the societal necessity of knowing what is right and what is wrong would very likely be the generation that destroyed the society. Of course, a small 10-year-old boy doesn't understand these concepts and probably would not understand even if explained in excruciating historical detail with examples. Hence, it became necessary to explain in a simple, more direct language.

However, I digress. The small Baptist church that became such a part of my young life was in itself quite unspectacular. It had started among a group of people who, like so many others before them, wanted to experience worship in a sense of freedom more to their understanding of the concept of praise and reverence. In my humble opinion, they succeeded quite well. Over the years, families came and went; there were births and deaths, marriages and widows and widowers, brotherhood and conflict, struggles and victories.

All of that took place year in and year out under the steeple of that small church. It was a simple structure. As young boys, we often wondered why there was no cross on the steeple. There was indeed something up there, but it appeared to be more of a lightning rod than a religious symbol. It was not until some many years later when the steeple was removed for repair that it became clear what the strange object was. Somehow, among all of the people who worked and sacrificed to build that small church, they had come to an agreement that the copper ball from a toilet tank would be an acceptable steeple topper.

War Stories from the Other Side

Before you read this, let me make a few things perfectly clear. I have the utmost respect for anyone who wears the military uniform of the United States. I believe they have been entrusted with one of the greatest human responsibilities that exist on this planet: to safeguard freedom, anywhere and everywhere it is threatened. Whether it is freedom for the citizens of the United States or the cause of freedom throughout the world, theirs is a most daunting task.

But like every other organization, there are those who carry the burden of battle and those who support the ones who carry the fight to the enemy. I was one of those "from the other side" who served my time in a support role. There was nothing noteworthy about my time in the U.S. Army, other than I made myself available and went and did what was asked of me.

Dad, Mom, and little brother, circa 1970 when my Army career began.

Soldiers and Drink

There is something about being in the army that causes men to drink. It could be that it is the thought that has finally struck home that the Army needs young men to engage and fight an enemy force. It is a known fact that young men die in combat. When this finally sinks in, young soldiers abandon a lot of their self-control.

Vic drank. Whatever it was that he drank made him cry. Or maybe, it was the drink that broke down the system that held back the crying. However it happened, sitting in the corner of the barracks and crying after a night of drink was always the last scene before his collapse and much needed rest.

I was 17 at the time, struggling through U.S. Army basic training at Ft. Polk, Louisiana. Though I had never been rich, I somehow managed, through a lack of expensive vices, to end the month with money. One dreary, rainy Saturday, Vic convinced me to lend him five dollars. After swearing he would not use it to buy booze, I relented and gave him the money.

I returned later that evening to find him sitting predictably in the corner near his cot, wailing and gasping for air. He apologized profusely, but I decided then that I would never again give him money. Somehow, for the remainder of our time together, he never again came back drunk. We were together for only 8 weeks, but I sometimes think of Vic and wonder if he is still alive. The odds would say no, but then again, there is hope.

CHRIS LOVED VODKA. Vodka hated Chris. It displayed that disdain by causing his eyelids to swell shut. After a half pint, he looked like a boxer who had best stayed out of the ring. To make matters worse, he drank at night and couldn't see to get back to the barracks in the dark.

I was a tea-totaler. Because of a common love for ham radio, and the commonality of California (both he and my mom were from California), a strange kind of friendship developed between us. I guess it is possible I might have been this nation's first designated walker. Chris would invite me to go with him whenever he had planned a night of drink. It wouldn't take very long before he would turn in my direction with eyes swollen shut and announce to me that he had had enough. I would walk him back to the barracks, see him to bed, and retire for the evening.

However he found the strength, he would be gone the next morning before I would awaken and return bright as the proverbial "penny in the well." I later learned that he would awaken, dress for walking, and walk the train tracks that passed outside the base into the next town, have breakfast and return. It was nearly 14 miles round trip.

Some Have Already Served

Ralph was nuts. What amazed me about his nuttiness was that the Army, in all of its pre-enlistment screening activities, did not detect it. Eight weeks of basic training, another six months of advanced individual training and yet he arrived on duty at Ft. Hood, Texas certifiably nuts.

Ralph was also one of the best guitar players I have ever met. He was just absolutely great. Because the army didn't recognize the guitar as a legitimate marching band instrument, he also played saxophone. He was a modest sax player. However, when the time came for the dance band scene (where he was permitted to play guitar), Ralph rose to new heights.

What made him nuts was that he was convinced he had been a U.S. Army general in a former life (swore he served under George S. Patton) and was therefore entitled to skip army duty in his present life. Knowing that the army would never buy such a story, he compensated himself by dressing in his former rank on weekends. He must have also been a drinking general in his previous life, for the uniform with the two silver stars never appeared until after a few cans of moderately cold beer had disappeared.

On one particularly brisk winter evening in late 1970, Ralph emerged from the latrine in full attire. He had such a commanding presence that I rose instinctively from my cot and drew myself to full attention before realizing it was Ralph. He promptly accepted my reaction with an official 'At ease, soldier.' turned, and with highly polished shoes clicking commandingly on the waxed floor, left the barracks.

I thought no more about Ralph until later that night when I was awakened from a full sleep by the sound of doors slamming and the rush of military shoes across the highly polished floor. It was immediately followed by the sound of someone undressing most hastily, a slam of a locker door, some muttered cursing, and the noise that only a body slamming into an army cot can produce. Before I could arise and investigate, the barracks door burst open and three puffing MPs hurled themselves into the room, turned on the lights, and demanded to know if a drunken general had just come in. Not having to pretend I had been asleep, and Ralph, being as good an actor as an idiot, the MPs soon retreated without finding their general.

Ralph had a very intense headache the next day.

Ken

Ken was from Kentucky, Paducah to be exact. If you ever thought you might know how someone would sound with a distinctive Southern drawl, Ken fit the bill. He was perfect for the mounted band as he had a terrible limp. One could even say he was physically handicapped.

How he got into the army was always an unsolved mystery to me. His right foot was turned outward at a very obvious angle, and he walked on the inside of his foot. The knee of that same leg turned inward at the same incredible angle. It appeared that it might have been broken at some time and mended poorly. However odd and out of place it seemed for a U.S. soldier, we had seen so much army absurdity that we never openly questioned it. He played trombone and with that leg, the jeep mounted marching unit was a perfect fit.

I mentioned he lived in Paducah. He loved his family dearly. When he would go on leave, he would drive home nonstop so as not to miss any leave time with his family. When leave was over, he would load his car with his belongings and four flasks of coffee. Being that he would remain at home until he had only driving time plus one hour left on his leave, he planned everything for the trip allowing only for stops for gasoline; no rest was planned or needed. The gasoline stops were carefully calculated down to the minute to align with his anticipated bathroom needs based on his rate of coffee consumption.

So, it was always a treat for everyone to meet outside the barracks just as his leave was about to expire and await his return. Sure enough, with only minutes to spare, he would come roaring up in the old Chevy, stumble out, and with a big toothy grin, announce his return. What made it most noteworthy was that the four flasks of coffee had been consumed in less than a day and that Ken was now set for two days without sleep.

Texas Bugle Duty

I played trumpet in the army. I've mentioned that already; but there were some unbelievable times that bore witness to the amazing majesty of human character. In addition to parades, changes of command, and retirement ceremonies, as a trumpeter, I was part of a rotating shift of about six others who had the duty of playing Taps at military funerals. We each pulled a week of standby duty in the event a military funeral was to take place. It was standard fare for retirees and those killed in action to receive a seven-man rifle squad with squad leader and a bugler for military graveside honors.

The standard routine involved checking out a 10-passenger van and leaving Ft. Hood early enough in the morning to drive up to several hours in time to arrive at some cemetery devoid of living people. We would often drive for hours traveling in the company of our individual thoughts, wondering about the life that had just been lost.

There was always a sort of indescribable nervousness about whether we would arrive on time, find the right cemetery, make the necessary connections with the local funeral director, and still manage to perform in an honorable fashion worthy of the sacrifice that had just been made.

The routine was pretty standard fare. After the appropriate messages and words of comfort and the presentation of the flag, the funeral director would signal the rifle squad leader who would direct the seven-man squad to fire three volleys, thus rendering a 21-gun salute. Immediately after they ordered arms, the bugler would deliver the final salute with Taps.

The rifle squad was always positioned within sight of the family, but the standard operating procedure was for the bugler to be out of sight and some distance from the mourners. The intent was to deliver a sort of message of comfort that someone unseen and distant cared for the soul that was lost. For the bugler, it was a blessing, because more time than not, the sounds of weeping and wailing would create such a state of nervousness that it rendered the bugler nearly out of control. The result would be a version of Taps played with a combination of uncontrollable vibrato and several cracked or sour notes.

When properly delivered, it really was quite impressive to hear the sound of the bugle drifting across a large cemetery, echoing off the hills and tombstones, and giving the effect of coming from everywhere simultaneously.

So, for the bugler, it became his responsibility to seek out a tree or large tombstone where he would remain out of sight until needed. At which time, he would play slowly and respectfully and deliver an appropriate honor, all the while remaining hidden to the mourners.

And so it was, one late, clear, morning somewhere in central Texas. We rarely knew very much about the KIA but would sometime get some insight into the soldier and surviving family from the funeral director, especially if he had experience with military funerals and was inclined to discuss the arrangements. In this particular case, the soldier was a young black man of 18. He had been drafted, sent to Vietnam, and died in combat only a few weeks after arriving in country. It all seemed such a waste, but we soldiers had learned almost immediately that it did little good to question.

We soon positioned ourselves and waited for the mourners to arrive. I watched from behind a large solitary tree about 75 yards from the gravesite as the large black hearse arrived and slowly came to rest near the freshly dug earth. A few dozen cars followed and after they had come to rest, their passengers soon positioned themselves in a semi-circle around the grave, with their backs to me.

I felt confident about this one. I waited patiently as the preacher delivered a message that I couldn't hear. I had a good sense about the timing, for people rarely want to spend very much time in cemeteries. I watched as the funeral director nodded to the squad leader who called the squad to attention. This was the moment when everything tensed, for in a few short seconds, out of sight or not, all ears would be on me. Even as I write this some 52 years later, I find my heartbeat speeding up, my throat tightening a bit as I swallow, and a very familiar feeling in my stomach.

The three volleys were delivered with precision. As soon as the echoes died down, I lifted my trumpet and began to play. No sooner had I played the first phrase than I heard the shrieking and wailing commence. It struck me like a hammer, but I continued on, intent to honor this fellow soldier to the best of my ability.

As I hit the high, sustained note and started down the phrase, I noticed out of the corner of my eye, a great commotion near the grave, and what appeared to be several people giving aid to someone who had collapsed. I ended as best as possible and remained out of sight.

Seeing what had transpired and that our part of the service was finished, the squad leader ordered his men to turn about face and marched them toward me and the van that we had parked some one hundred yards behind me. I joined them when they passed the tree and silently, we made our way to the van. Convinced that we had performed well and that our work was done, we broke the formation when we were confident we were well out of sight.

It was always a sense of relief when it was over, and the smokers immediately reached for their comfort. I proceeded to put the trumpet away and loosen the necktie. In a few moments, we would be gone, and the day would soon blend with the others that had passed.

It was no secret that the Vietnam War was unpopular with a large percentage of African Americans. The draft of the early 1970's often took those who couldn't find an alternative like college or Canada, and it was a generally acknowledged fact that black soldiers fared worse.

So, you can imagine the sense of dread that came upon me when I looked back toward the gravesite and saw five of the biggest black men I had ever seen coming across the cemetery in our direction with a walk that cried out with purpose. I looked at the squad leader who looked at the squad who looked at me. Without a word, it was generally agreed that we could jump in the van and get away before they could close the last few yards, but for some reason, we felt it best to stand our ground and endure the outcome.

My heart was pounding as they stopped a few feet in front of us. I had already decided to take the first punch and drop to the ground. My feeble brain had decided that since they were outnumbered, if I dropped out of the fight, my attacker would probably turn to help his friends, thus sparing me a merciless beating.

What happened next completely floored me. The man in the middle stepped forward and announced in a strong but shaky Texan voice, "Mama says ya gotta come by the house and get somethin' to eat."

To say we were relieved was an understatement. We took their instructions and soon found ourselves at a very simple and humble house some six or seven miles from the cemetery. There was food everywhere, and even more people than had been at the gravesite. We ate until we could hold nothing else.

I had positioned myself against a post near the far end of the porch and listened as discretely as I could to the conversation surrounding the fallen soldier's mother who was seated in an old rocking chair just beside the door. Everyone presented themselves to express their sorrow for her loss and to remind her of their love for her and their promises of help.

The more I listened, the more I learned. She had born seven sons. One had died in a car accident some years earlier and now she had lost a second. I learned that she had buried her husband some years back and that the fallen soldier had been laid to rest right next to his father.

I eventually found out that the commotion at the grave had been her father who had collapsed at the sound of the bugle. I wanted to shrink from sight, but since I had not been seen, I felt I would be safe to just sit and finish my banana pudding. We eventually expressed our gratitude and asked to be excused as we had a decent drive to get back to base.

To this day, I will never forget the last words I heard the widowed woman say to us as we started toward the van.

"God has been so good to me. Thank you for coming." The trip back to base was nearly completely silent.

Looking back, I was glad this happened early in my military career. From that day forward, every funeral became more than simple duty. Despite the distance between gravesite and my hideaway across the cemetery, I always knew there were other mothers, brothers, grandfathers, and friends whose faces I could not see, but to whom I was connected in an indescribable way.

Okinawa Bugle Duty

The U.S. Army soon found it wise to send me overseas. Fortunately, the trip stopped at a small island off the South China Sea, and I never made it the rest of the way to Vietnam. It was a mostly unknown place at my time in history named Okinawa, where a previous generation had fought, died, and laid its dead to rest with rifle squad and bugler.

Because Okinawa was relatively near to Vietnam, the army had assembled a graveyard there for vehicles damaged in combat. The intention was to remove as much useable material from the vehicles as possible and use it to repair the less severely damaged. These would then be shipped back across the sea to Vietnam.

I would often spend a full Saturday wandering through the acres of evidence of the brutality of battle. I remember the frequency of which I would find bullet holes in the big white star that was painted so prominently on the door of the big trucks. I still wonder about who was sitting on the other side of those doors and if the penetrating bullets ended their lives. Somewhere in America, some of those drivers were laid to rest with the notes of a hidden bugler.

THE OKINAWA PATCH IS in the middle. The symbol represents the Torii gate.

One of many long-standing traditions still being observed in today's Army is Retreat. Retreat is a ceremony that honors the U.S. flag when it is lowered in the evening, usually at 5 p.m.

The term Retreat is taken from the French word "Retraite" and refers to the evening ceremony. The bugle call sounded at Retreat was first used in the French Army and dates back to the Crusades. Retreat was sounded at sunset to notify sentries to start challenging until sunrise, and to tell the rank and file to go to their quarters.

Today, the observance of Retreat signifies retirement of the colors from the day's activities. Retreat is announced by bugle call, followed by the firing of the ceremonial cannon and the playing of "To the Colors," music honoring the flag as it is lowered in the evening.

The observance of Retreat requires the rendering of some common courtesies by all personnel, military, civilian employees, and civilian guests on post.

While I was there in Okinawa, I shared bugle duty with four fellow trumpeters. Every afternoon for one week out of the month, one of us would travel by Japanese taxi to HQ and play *Retreat* and *To the Colors* for the lowering of the flag at 5:00 p.m. Excuse me, I err; it should be 1700 hrs.

It was okay duty, not demanding in any way and somewhat fun in that the routine involved the firing of a cannon. To be more precise, it was a 105mm cannon, perched next to the flagpole on the highest spot of that part of the island. It looked out over the city of Sukiran, which allowed the sound of the cannon to be heard quite easily by soldiers everywhere. The idea was that no matter where a soldier was, he could hear the cannon and stand to attention. I had seen drivers pull off the road, exit their automobiles, and pull themselves erectly to attention and salute in the direction of the flag.

THE CANNON WOULD BE fired by members of the Military Police unit who would arrive at 4:55, take their positions at the flagpole and beside the 105. They brought with them a single cylinder, a blank shell, which provided the noise and smoke for the cannon. The cannoneer would place the shell gently into the chamber and take hold of the lanyard in preparation for the ceremony.

Now just as a reminder, the observance of Retreat requires the rendering of some common courtesies by all personnel, military, civilian employees and civilian guests on post. Personnel in uniform were to face in the direction of the flag (or direction from which the music emanates if the flag is not in view) and stand at attention. After the cannon fires and at the first note of "To the Colors," they are to render hand salute. *They hold this position until the last note of music has played.*

On two separate occasions, I broke the observance and failed my country and my honor.

One of the things I had not been introduced to as a young boy in South Louisiana was dental floss. I paid dearly for it. By the time I was in high school, I had endured some of the most intense pain known to humankind: the toothache and the trip to the dentist without the benefit of painkillers. So, you can imagine my joy at learning that in Okinawa, Army dentists used anesthetics. I made an initial visit and set up a schedule to get every problem in my mouth taken care of. Not knowing all of the duty days for bugling, I accepted the appointments offered by the receptionist and began my monthly visits.

All worked out well for a while until there was a change in personnel and the bugle duty rotation shifted. It turned out that a dentist appointment and bugle duty fell on the same day in late 1971. The appointment was early in the morning and duty late in the afternoon. I was certain the anesthetic would wear off by the time of Retreat, so I made no arrangements for someone to take my place. Even as I sat in the taxi, I was still certain I could play. I buzzed my lips, moved my tongue about, and reassured myself that all was well.

As we came to attention at the flagpole, the MP in charge gave me the signal to go ahead. I raised the trumpet to my lips and the first note sounded like something emanating from a cow giving birth. I tried again. Still nothing. I looked at the MP who signaled the cannoneer who fired the cannon. Being high on the hill, the cannon sounded out clearly across the base. I can still imagine the confusion as personnel everywhere came to attention, saluted, and held the salute waiting for the end of the music that never started.

The second time was not my fault. It was a Monday. My lips were in fine form. We arrived well in advance of the ceremony and took our places. At the appointed time, I played Retreat. The MP in charge gave the signal to the cannoneer, who pulled dutifully on the lanyard. The 105 responded and let loose with the expected loud blast and puff of smoke.

What was not expected was what flew out of the end of the barrel. For now, drifting slowly down upon the city was a collection of "stuff." I played as best as I could, all the while looking out past the end of my trumpet at the seemingly endless rain of empty beer cans, ribbons of toilet paper, and various other articles slowly disappearing out of sight. The absurdity of it eventually got the best of me. I finally broke into an uncontrollable smile that soon deteriorated into a chuckle that eventually ended the rendition of *To the Colors*.

The best the MPs could determine was that some drunken soldier had apparently spent a rather disgusting weekend of drinking and figured the cannon barrel would be a good place to hide his cans. For good measure, he threw in a couple of rolls of toilet paper and whatever else he could scrounge. We were grateful that he had not chosen to slip a few full cans into the mix. Someone could have been seriously hurt.

Texas Parades

Texas is a patriotic state. Every town has a Fourth of July parade and barbecue. To be invited to participate in a Texas parade and subsequent BBQ feast was noteworthy and memorable. One of the remarkable things about a Texas BBQ in 1970 was the fact that it was a certain place where you did not need to feel embarrassed or ashamed of being in the military. I recall quite vividly being reminded that the short haircut could often get you the brunt of a verbal attack by those who opposed the war. You never felt that threat at a Texas BBQ.

WHILE I WAS AT FT. Hood, I was a member initially of the First Armored Division and later the First Cavalry Division bands. What made these bands memorable was that they were the only vehicle-mounted band in the free world at that time. We would sit two to three musicians per jeep with a driver and depending upon the width of the parade route, 3 to 6 jeeps across and 3 to 6 jeeps deep. It made quite an impressive sight coming down the street.

Every Texas parade has horses. Not just the two in the front near the flags, but the local 4-H club, the local boarding ranch, the cattleman's association, the Sheriff's Search and Rescue, the Texas Ladies Riding Club, the Young Texas Ladies Riding Club, and on and on. Sitting high in our jeeps, we were grateful to be immune to the countless pasture patties left on the Texas streets during these parades.

One year we were invited to take part in the 4th of July parade in Dallas. Being that it was such a big parade, the armored Division decided to go all out and send a few battle tanks to join us in a particularly impressive display of military hardware. We made our way up there on the day of the parade and positioned ourselves near the rear of the lineup. The tanks were placed in front of the band so their noise would have passed by and our music could be heard as we moved down the parade route.

The M60 main battle tank was made for combat. It is a huge beast designed for the possibility of conflict in Eastern Europe. It was never meant for parade duty in the streets of Dallas, Texas. As is sometimes the case, there are mechanical problems with tanks. The lead tank was having some sort of problem that caused it to fall behind the rest of the parade, so much so that its driver eventually lost sight of the parade when it turned onto a side street. As we approached the street where the driver thought he had seen the parade turn, he turned, and we followed.

Before even one block, the whole convoy came to a stop. Eventually we stopped playing and our commander descended from the lead jeep and made his way to the tank to see about the problem. He soon returned and announced that the lead tank had indeed taken a wrong turn and was now firmly lodged in the narrowing street between an abandoned warehouse and the rear of a small restaurant.

It was not the Army's finest hour.

Afterthought

I saw an old man walking today. He was dressed against the cold: John Deere cap, plaid flannel jacket, woolen gloves, and sports shoes. I assumed he was walking for fitness, although it was pretty evident that he would not be setting any speed or endurance records. He shuffled along, head bowed, looking mostly at the ground. I wondered what he was thinking as he moved up the sidewalk past the high school. Perhaps he was deep in thought of some long-past fond memory or maybe some recent tragic event.

He paused momentarily, turned slowly, and looked up into the sky. He watched silently as the big jet airplane scrolled slowly across the clear blue, laboring under its load of Fed-Ex cargo. As it passed out of view, he once again lowered his head, turned, and continued his journey. Even in their old age, boys are still mesmerized by the same things that captivated them when they could run across the hills. I wonder if he had a window fan when his family was young.

Also by Wiley Traylor

The Strange Tale of Billy McGinty
The Porches of 101 North Pine Street
Isaiah's Farm
We Had a Window Fan
The Ordinary Life of Anderson Lane

About the Author

Wiley Traylor is an amateur writer who writes for fun. Born a long time ago in a small town in Louisiana, he now abides in Tennessee where he spends his retirement thinking about and writing stories of adventure with an element of mystery and developing characters whom he would like to meet one day.